"No cell phone No way"

By Grace Bogart

AuthorHouse™
1663 Liberty Drive
Bloomington, IN 47403
www.authorhouse.com
Phone: 1 (800) 839-8640

Published by AuthorHouse 07/18/2019

ISBN: 978-1-7283-1913-1 (sc)
ISBN: 978-1-7283-1914-8 (hc)
ISBN: 978-1-7283-1915-5 (e)

authorHOUSE®

I would like to thank Pearl Alba of author house for her ever giving patience and guidance. My husband for faithfully reading every rough draft. My son Anthony for the little heart he drew on my finished manuscript And Everyone for there encouragement (there are to many to list but I hope you know who you are)

And of course my granddaughter Baily. This book would NOT exist without you.

"**N**o cell phone, no way!" Bailey shouted.

"I'm sorry, Bailey. You'll have to wait till we get to the cottage. We have a charger there," Grandma said.

Bailey huffed. Looking out the window, she spotted a cat rubbing against a rocker on the porch of an old house. The cat was gray with white paws that reminded her of mittens. *How cute*, she thought.

In the car next to them, two girls sat in the back and were glued to their phones.

"They're so lucky. I'm so mad right now!" Bailey cried out.

"Now, Bailey Boo," Grandpa said.

"Don't call me Bailey Boo. It's Bailey Lou!" Bailey shouted.

As they entered the expressway, there were tall weeds on each side of the road. While she was gazing at the weeds, she saw something popping in and out of them. She blinked to clear her eyes, because she didn't believe what she saw, but there they were tiny fairies. Quite pretty except for their long, pointed noses; their eyes were crossed too. They were flying every which way and bumping into each other. Bailey giggled when she saw one fly out and smack into a tree. There seemed to be hundreds of them.

Above the weeds, coming closer and closer were three airplanes—they didn't look like ordinary planes though. The face of the plane had a creepy smile and evil-looking, slanted windows where the pilot and copilot sat. The steel wings flapped up and down gracefully at the sides of the vessel. Above the wings were narrow windows exposing what looked to be passengers. One plane, however, was heading right toward them. Bailey gasped.

"That was close. The plane must be coming in for a landing. It just skimmed over the roof of the car," Grandpa said.

But passing the city airport, Bailey thought it was weird because all these planes looked normal.

Just past the airport on the right of the expressway was a lake in which a man was fishing. He looked bored.

"He probably wishes he had his cell phone," Bailey mumbled to herself.

The water started stirring a little, then a lot! Massive waves began to form. The waves were going crazy—so crazy in fact that Bailey lost sight of the man. She glanced out the back window and caught sight of him surfing on a wave. He looked at her and winked.

Turning back around, Bailey spotted a bright light shining through the fast-approaching trees. A magnificent buck creeped out of the woods. A brilliant glow radiated from him. His piercing blue eyes were glaring right at her. He followed them, running swiftly through the trees.

"Bailey, would you like some gummies and some bottled water?" Grandma asked.

"Sure," Bailey said.

Grandma handed her a plastic bag with all different flavors of gummies. They seemed to have way more flavor than she remembered. The green ones were lime flavored, which made her face pucker up. The orange ones tasted as if she was eating an actual orange. Her favorite, though, were the red ones, fruit punch.

"Yummy! These are great," Bailey mumbled as she chewed.

Grandma laughed. "Those are the same kind I always bring."

Bailey tried twisting the cap off the water bottle.

"Remember, lefty loosey, righty tighty," grandma said.

Bailey turned the cap hard. Snap! She took a big gulp. She looked down and saw roads looping in and out of each other. *They look like a giant roller coaster*, she thought.

Bailey's heart started racing as Grandpa took the winding roads that went up, over, and down the giant bridge. She held her breath as an enormous bright-red semi came up alongside them.

The clouds were moving fast. They went from white cotton balls to dirty-gray ones. Flashes of light and loud booms were coming from the sky. The rain started. *Tap, tap, tap, swish, swish, boom.* Bailey started to bob left and right. Suddenly, her whole body started rocking to the sounds of the rain and windshield wipers.

The car started hydroplaning over the wet pavement, which sent shivers down her spine. The rain faded as the sun started to shine.

Out the front window were humongous pinwheels that must have been thirty feet tall with three ten-foot spikes sticking out of the circle in the center. There were miles of them.

"What are those?" Bailey asked.

"Those are windmills. They create electricity. I'm surprise you never noticed them!" Grandpa said.

"Those don't look like windmills to me," Bailey said. As she stared at them, she started to see creepy faces in the centers of the windmills. She wondered if they were really aliens coming to invade our planet. The spikes were moving around the faces of the windmills. *I bet they're checking out the atmosphere,* Bailey thought.

They drove past a billboard showing kids at a waterpark. Bailey imagined herself going down the slide and splashing into the water. She asked her grandpa if they could go there sometime.

"Sure, Bailey Boo," Grandpa said with a grin.

"Stop calling me that!" Bailey yelled.

There was another billboard showing cops eating doughnuts.

"I wish I had a doughnut," Bailey said.

"I was thinking the same thing," Grandpa said.

They exited the expressway, and Grandpa pulled into the gas station. While he was pumping gas, Bailey saw a flock of birds flying overhead. She was envisioning herself flying with them, swooping through the sky, when suddenly one of the birds wrapped its wings around her and they started tumbling to the ground! Bailey gasped.

Slam! Grandpa slammed the car door and got in.

As they drove through the city, Bailey could smell fudge, which made her mouth water.

Grandpa pulled up in front of the doughnut shop. There were people taking pictures of their heads in big holes in a huge billboard that made them look as if they were being taken away by the cops.

Grandpa asked what kind of doughnuts they would like. Bailey wanted the raspberry-filled with the icing on the top, of course. Grandma wanted the glazed.

They passed the putt-putt golf course where they had once played.

"I was the best putt-putt player ever," Bailey said with pride.

Grandpa and Grandma smiled and talked about Bailey picking up the balls and running all over the place.

"We're almost there," Grandpa said.

The ride seemed a lot shorter than Bailey had expected. They passed a farm with a broken-down old barn. The wood was a faded gray, and the door was hanging half off the hinges. It was all dark and spooky. She just knew someone was lurking inside! After taking the winding country road, she spotted the cottage. They pulled into the driveway.

"I'll plug your cell phone into the charger," Grandma told her.

"Thanks, Grandma. Actually, the ride was kind of awesome without it."

They hadn't been in the cabin but a minute when there was a knock on the door.

It was Vic, who was visiting his grandparents across the road.

"Do you want to go on an adventure?" Vic asked.

"Sure," Bailey replied.

The leaves started blowing as Vic shut the door. "Don't step on them!" Vic shouted.

Bailey looked down. The leaves were turning into field mice, which scampered all around them. They started hopping over the mice to avoid crushing them beneath their feet. A huge blackbird came swooping down and landed right in front of them.

Vic introduced them. "Bailey Lou, this is Larry LaRue."

"Why, how do you do Bailey Lou?" the bird bellowed.

"Ah, you actually talk?" Bailey asked.

"Ah yeah," Vic said. "He's my best friend when you're not around."

"While I was daydreaming on the way to the cottage, did you wrap your wings around me, causing us both to tumble to the ground?" Bailey asked.

"It was me," Larry said.

"Don't you know you have to spread your wings to fly?" Bailey yelled.

"Don't yell at him. He was protecting you," Vic yelled back at her.

"I know how long I can go without spreading my wings before we crash," Larry said.

"What were you protecting me from?" Bailey asked.

"From the rays," Larry said as he flew away.

"What rays?" Bailey asked Vic.

"I didn't know about the rays till now. Earlier today he said he protected you from something. He didn't tell me what it was." Vic shrugged.

"Look at those silly fairies in the weeds." Bailey giggled as she pointed at the bottom of the weeds.

"Don't laugh at them!" Vic shouted.

"But they look so silly bumping into each other. Their crossed eyes and those long, pointed noses look so ridiculous!" Bailey laughed.

"There's a reason they were born with crossed eyes and long, pointed noses. It's to save them from Venus flytraps."

Bailey noticed that baby Venus flytraps were snapping at the fairies.

"Their crossed eyes make them fly so wacko that the Venus flytraps can't catch them. Their long, pointed noses protect them against predators because at the end of their noses is itch serum. If you got pricked by one, you would itch for days. Look out!" Vic said.

A monstrous Venus flytrap was bending down, snapping at Bailey. The plants were lunging up all over.

"Cross your eyes and run!" Vic shouted.

They crossed their eyes and started running all wacko and screaming as loud as they could. A bright light was coming out of the trees ahead of them.

It was the magnificent, glowing buck Bailey had seen earlier. His piercing blue eyes were glaring at them. He gestured for them to hop on his back. Bailey helped Vic up.

"Don't look at him too long or you will go blind," Vic said.

They started weaving in and out of the trees.

"Ouch!" Vic exclaimed when one of the branches slapped him in the face.

The buck stopped in front of the dock. They slid off his back, and the deer ran off into the woods. Bailey followed Vic to the end of the dock.

"Do you want a piece of gum?" Vic asked.

"Sure," Bailey replied.

He handed her a piece of gum. "I'm sure you know all about the buck," Vic said smugly.

"No. What?" Bailey said anxiously.

"He was the most magnificent of all deer. His big brown eyes could spot a hunter any which way. His muscular legs could put the fastest of animal to shame, even the cheetah!"

"No way."

"All the hunters would brag that they would be the one to bring it down."

Vic blew a huge bubble that popped all over his face. Scraping the gum off his face, he continued. "One day around dusk, a kid was swimming in this here lake. The current started taking him deeper into the water, and he started screaming. The buck heard him, and since he was a strong swimmer, he leaped into the lake."

"I didn't know deer were strong swimmers," Bailey said while chomping on her gum.

"They're actually very strong swimmers," Vic replied. "Anyway, the deer pulled him to the dock with his teeth and pushed him up with his head to safety. But as the deer was getting out, he lost his footing and was caught up in the same current. It took him down. A few years later, sightings of a magnificent glowing deer with piercing blue eyes were reported throughout the town. That's why the lake is called Buck Lake."

Just as he was finishing the story, the dock started cracking away from the shore.

Chapter 4

"Do something!" Bailey shouted.

"Like what?" Vic cried.

There was a boat in the distance. As they started drifting toward it, Bailey recognized the man in the boat. It was the fisherman she had seen on the way up north.

"Pee-ew! What's that smell?" Vic said while holding his nose.

"Ahoy, mateys! Welcome aboard!" the man called out.

He was short and chubby with a white beard. He wore a fishing cap with fishing tackle tangled all over it. He had all kinds of fishing gear in the boat, and the smell was pretty bad, but they had no choice. They hopped in. He handed them each a fishing pole and pointed to a bucket of worms. They each took a worm out of the bucket and put them on their hooks.

"There now. Let's catch some fish!" the fisherman said.

They all drew their poles back and flung them into the water. Immediately, Bailey felt a tug on her line. She pulled up on it. To her surprise she saw a plaid fish dangling on the end.

"I caught a fish!" Vic shouted. His was green camouflage. "Cool!" Vic gasped.

Bailey peeked into the bucket they were told to put their catches into. There were two paisley, three argyle, two camouflage, and her plaid one in it. She thought they smelled like dirty socks.

"Let's eat!" the fisherman said cheerfully.

"We can actually eat them?" Bailey asked.

"Of course," he said. "But first we have to wash them."

There were three buckets. One for washing, one for rinsing, and one for eating.

The man took one fish and started singing. "Washy, washy, washy with a big loud cheer. Rinsey, rinsey, rinsey in the water so clear." Then he put the fish to his nose, took a big whiff, and said, "Hmm, smells like a rose." Then he tossed it into the bucket to eat. He picked up another one. "Washy, washy, washy with a big loud cheer. Rinsey, rinsey, rinsey in the water so clear." But when he put it to his nose this time, a disgusted look came over his face. "Pee-ew!" he exclaimed. His face turned red when he realized it was one of his socks he was smelling.

When all the fish were washed, he popped one into his mouth. "Yummy," he said.

"Don't you have to cook them before you eat them?" Bailey asked.

"No, they're much better raw. Here, try one," he said as he handed a fish to Vic.

"Ladies first," Vic said.

The man handed Bailey an argyle one.

She bit a piece of the tail off. "Yuck! Chocolate with peanut butter. I hate peanut butter!" Bailey bellowed.

"I'll take that one!" Vic shouted. "I love peanut butter."

The man passed a paisley one to Bailey. "Vanilla with butterscotch, yum! These are the best fish I've ever eaten," Bailey said.

All of a sudden a huge wave rocked the boat.

"Here she comes. Get back on the dock. I'll stay with the boat," the fisherman said.

Bailey and Vic both jumped onto the dock, and then they saw it: a gigantic catfish. Its whiskers were flapping all around it. It went straight up out of the water and then came plunging down, causing enormous waves. They balanced themselves on the dock and started riding the waves as if they were surfing.

"This is awesome!" Baily shouted.

"Yeah," Vick said shakily.

The waves stopped abruptly, causing the dock to crash right back where it broke off. They both went flying onto dry land.

"Are you all right?" Vic asked.

"Guess so," Bailey said.

They got up and wiped themselves off.

"I hope the fisherman is okay." Bailey was worried.

"Me too," Vic said. "We'd better head on home."

Bailey looked behind her. There was green slime oozing up over the shore. Bailey tugged on Vic's shirt.

Vic looked over at her.

She pointed at the sludge coming up.

"Run!" Vic shouted.

Bailey looked up and saw Larry LaRue flying overhead. He spread his wings and started flying higher and higher until she could no longer see him.

The wind started blowing harder and harder. Bailey grabbed onto a tree to keep from being blown away. Vic grabbed onto Bailey, and they both went sailing in midair. The force of the wind caused the slime to slither back into the lake. When there was no more sign of the slime, the wind stopped.

I just know Larry LaRue has magical powers, she thought.

"I was about to come looking for you two," Grandpa said. "Grandma said your cell phone is all charged."

"Thanks, Grandpa, but I'm exhausted," said Bailey. "We had our own amazing, awesome adventure without it."

Printed in the United States
By Bookmasters